ABSOLOOT PRESENTS

The Adventures of
JUNIOR & RUBBLE

THE OIL MONSTER-PART 1

Created by Ramon "Absoloot" Robinson.
Short story by Ramon "Absoloot" Robinson
and T.S. Witt.
Illustrations by Francis Llamzon

LIFE SPORTS FITNESS

2017

First Printing: 2017

Published by:
Ramon "Absoloot" Robinson
4716 West Atlantic Blvd, Apt 102
Coconut Creek, FL 33063
Tel: (954) 805-4391
www.antibullyingbuddy.com

Ordering Information:
Special discounts are available on quantity purchases by bookstores, wholesalers, corporations, associations, educators, and others. For details, contact the publisher at the above listed address.

PAGE 1

Junior lay in the shade with his dog Rubble lounging by his side. Rubble was a pure blooded American Akita, smart, fun, loving, but always on the lookout.

He and Junior found each other when they were both just kids. That's how Junior thought about it anyway. Now Rubble weighed as much as he did.

This was Junior's fourteenth birthday and he was enjoying the morning with Rubble, knowing that his mom had sent him outside so she could set up a surprise for him. She was always doing things like that.

Mom and Dad were proud Americans. They had left Haiti before Junior was born to come to the U.S. and worked hard to become citizens. Every year, there was a little flag on his cake to remind him he'd been born in the U.S.A.

PAGE 3

Junior smiled to himself and reached for Rubble. The earth beneath him trembled. They both became perfectly still. It trembled again. Junior began to feel sick. Suddenly, it was if he was back in that pile of broken concrete and rocks, struggling to free himself, coughing, crying out.

It was 2010 and Junior and his parents were visiting their relatives in Haiti when the earthquake hit. One minute he was playing with his cousins, the next, he was all alone in the rubble, terrified.

But then he heard whining and scratching. He wriggled around until he found where it was coming from and carefully started to dig. He hit rock and couldn't go any further.

RUMBLE
RUMBLE

:WHAT'S GOING ON?

DID THOSE ROCKS JUST MOVE ON THEIR OWN?

I FEEL FUNNY. AM I RUNNING OUT OF AIR?

PAGE 5

Junior was so frustrated, he balled up his fists and glared at the rocks. Two of the bigger ones slid apart just enough for Junior to get his hands through.

"What's going on? I feel funny. Am I running out of air?" Junior stared at the two rocks that had just seemed to move on their own. Then he heard the scratching again and started to dig between the rocks.

A fluffy white puppy's paw came through the little hole he made. Then a wet little nose snuffled at him. Junior dug and dug until his fingers hurt to free the little thing. It crawled into his arms and went straight to sleep. Strangely, Junior wasn't afraid anymore.

He fell asleep too.

Licking and tiny barks woke him. The puppy was bouncing around the little space they were in like it wanted to play. Its bushy tail was curled over its golden back and bounced right along with him.

"Sorry boy, we're stuck here. I can't even stand up." The seriousness of his situation hit Junior again. Tears filled his eyes.

The puppy barked at him several times, then started digging at the hole he had come in through. Junior didn't understand at first. Then he started digging too. The puppy must know the way out!

They dug together until Junior thought his arms would catch fire, they burned so much. He was afraid to try moving the rocks like before. He wasn't even sure he could. But he knew the whole opening might cave in on them if he moved the wrong rocks.

So they dug between the rubble and through the dirt. Then, just as he sat back to take a breath, he was blinded by a tiny shaft of sunlight. He started yelling and digging as hard as he could, the puppy right alongside him.

"We're here, we're here!"
he yelled. The puppy barked furiously.

Large hands broke through the wreckage, showering Junior with dirt and small chucks of debris. Then the hands pulled him out.

"Boy, we never would have heard you without that dog of yours." The owner of the large hands told him.
"You okay?"

"Yes," said Junior, looking around in horror at the devastation. "But I have to find my parents. And my cousins were right here with me when it hit." He picked up the puppy without thinking and started stroking him.

"We pulled three kids out of a shallow pit yesterday, just over there." The man pointed toward a hole in the floor of concrete, rocks and steel sheeting. "There's a board at the Red Cross tent with lists to help families find each other We'll take you there."

Junior climbed up into the big man's jeep. They had driven several miles when he started to feel upset, like he was missing something very important. The puppy began to bark like crazy.

"Stop, stop the jeep!" he cried, jumping before it had even come to a stop.

PAGE 13

Junior ran out into the rocks and broken trees and overturned cars and started yelling for his parents. The puppy stopped barking. He put his nose to the ground and sniffed, running around in a figure eight. Junior yelled, "Over here! Over here!"

The big man and his two friends came running. They started pulling off tree limbs and tires and tin sheets until they hit dirt. Then they all dug. They hit rock, but it moved easily without the dirt on top of it. There, in a small hole made by some tree trunks and rocks, huddled together were Junior's parents. It was then Junior knew Rubble was special.

"Oh Junior, you're safe!" His mother started to cry hysterically. His father helped her up and after much hugging and kissing – by his mom – they all went to the Red Cross tent to find the rest of the family. Everyone was safe.

WHAT IS THAT!?

YOU WILL NOT HARM ANOTHER ANIMAL ON THIS BEACH!

PAGE 15

Then he saw it, a long black finger of oil creeping up the beach near his house, heading straight for a little shorebird's nest. Could he get there in time? How would he stop it? Junior worried as he ran toward the thing.

Rubble began to bark, running ahead, his webbed toes giving him good traction in the sand. The tiny mama bird huddled further into the dried grass and broken shells of her nest, trying to hide from the thing coming toward her. Junior ran past a large sand dune that was blocking his view of part of the Gulf of Mexico and stopped dead in his tracks.

A huge, black oil monster with five long tentacles was laying out in the ocean, reaching in for the shore. It swelled and undulated with the waves.

It had already caught an otter at the mouth of a small inlet farther down the beach.

Junior became furious. That oil would seriously harm the birds and animals that lived and fished on the Gulf coast. He had to do something. He balled up his fists.

"You will not harm another animal on this beach!" Junior challenged. The sand and water rose up like a wave and swallowed the tentacle that had been reaching for the little bird. The sand wave rolled the oil into a harmless tar ball that could be picked up and safely disposed of. The monster swelled up in the water as if in pain.

"Whoa! Did I do that?" Junior looked at Rubble in astonishment.

SPLASH
SPLASH
SPLASH

PAGE 19

But he didn't have time to worry or be afraid, the little otter needed help. He stroked Rubble and thought of rocks. Junior concentrated on the
tentacle holding the poor otter.

A sharp sheet of shale, two inches thick and three feet wide, shot up out of the inlet and sliced that tentacle in two. The otter struggled to shore and lay still, breathing hard.The oil monster split its broken

tentacle down the middle and tried to go around the shale rock, but Junior's hand was still on Rubble.
He began to hear tiny little sounds in the surf, hungry sounds. He called to those little creatures with
all his might.

PAGE 21

They were natural oil-eating bacteria that lived in the sea. Junior had just learned about them in school, and memorized the name, Alcanivorax Borkumensis.

And they came.

They came in numbers so great that the oil monster pulled back all its tentacles. It tried to move out to sea, but the bacteria were faster. They gobbled the monster up within minutes.Junior stood looking out at the sparkling water in amazement.

Rubble whined.

"What is it boy?" Junior turned to follow the big dog's gaze.

PAGE 23

The poor little otter was still covered in oil and struggling to move. Junior ran to his house and called for help. He knew that there were people who could clean the otter up quickly and make him better. And Junior needed to find out where that oil monster had come from.

He was also crazy tired. He leaned on Rubble and felt a bit better.

Closing his eyes, he saw the golden raintree his parents
planted outside his bedroom window when they returned from Haiti in 2010.

It was seven years old, just like Rubble. Weird.

He stepped back outside and walked around the house. When he reached the tree, he knew what he needed. He put both hands on the slender trunk and took deep breaths.

With every breath he felt stronger and stronger.

This was getting stranger by the minute! He needed to get his head around this, but first, some water. Man, was he thirsty.

As soon as he walked back into the house, his parents yelled, "Surprise!"

They jumped out of the kitchen with their neighbors and several of his friends from school. "Happy birthday, Junior!"

Junior smiled. There, in his father's hands, was a cake with fourteen candles and an American flag on it.

He made a wish, a secret wish. He wished to understand what had happened today and for whatever it was to help him find out who had made that oil monster.

After the party, Junior set out for the beach. His two best friends, Jack and Seth, wanted to come along. He couldn't tell them no, so he told them the truth. Most of it anyway.

"So this morning, me and Rubble saw some oil in the Gulf." Junior began.

"No way!" Seth's whole body tensed. Even his wavy hair looked stiff with anger.

"Yea, it's gone now, but I really want to know where it came from. An otter got covered with it. You guys want to help?" Junior almost hoped they'd say no.

PAGE 29

He had no idea what was happening to him. It was like when he was a little kid back in the earthquake in Haiti, only stronger. But, he couldn't tell anyone, not even the guys. He didn't want any trouble for his parents. They were legal citizens, but they were still immigrants. Sometimes that mattered to other people.

"Of course we do." Jack grinned. "Sounds like an adventure to me." He was always up for a bit of fun. And he thought most things were fun.

Seth slapped Junior on the back. "Count me in." Junior smiled at his two friends. They really were the best. He hated keeping secrets from them. But for now, he was just going to have to be careful.

Rubble nuzzled Junior's hand and tucked his big head under Junior's arm. He looked down at Rubble. Together, Junior knew they would find the culprit.